NOXIOUS

Was it Love or *Poison?*

By: Pamela James Coleman

S.H.E. PUBLISHING, LLC

For information contact: www.shepublishingllc.com
info@shepublishingllc.com

Cover Design by Pamela James Coleman
Finding Your Path | Life Coaching in Charlottesville
https://findingyourpath.info

ISBN: 978-1-953163-77-6

First Edition: May 2023

10 9 8 7 6 5 4 3 2 1

Contents

Introduction

Knock knock.
Knock, knock, knock.

"What the hell?"

"I know he hears me!"

"I know he is there; I hear music."

Harper turns the doorknob, it is unlocked. She walks in, the table is set for their date. Music is playing, Justice is nowhere in sight.

The music is coming from the back of the apartment, Harper starts to walk in the direction of the music. The closer she gets to the door, the more she realizes this might not be a promising idea.

She stands at the door, on the other side, sounds of someone other than Justice. Harper opens the door, with pain in her heart, there's Justice with three other women in the bed. Harper stands there for what seems to be forever, watching them. There was Justice being pleasured by three women, Harper gasped for air, all four of them stop what they were doing to see her standing in the doorway.

Harper reaches into her bag, grabs her gun as Justice is crawling to the edge of the bed saying it's not what you think. With the gun placed in the middle of Justice forehead, she replied, this is not what YOU THINK! The gun goes off.

How did I get here?

CHAPTER 1

Harper & Andi

Sunrises through the blinds shining into Harper's face. She looks to her left, to see no one lying in the bed next to her. It has been two years since her husband has died, she is starting to notice the void of her husband not being there.

She begins her day as normal, coffee, shower, her music blasting, with her dancing around the room. With her morning routine complete, it is time for her to head off to work. She works for the local school system. She loves her job and the people she works with.

This day will be different for Harper, when she arrives to work, her friend Andi was at the door waiting to greet.

"Hey girl, Happy Monday to you." Andi said.

"Ok, what trouble are we about to get into?" was Harper's response.

"Don't make any plans tonight." Remarked Andi.

"Should I be afraid?" Harper said?

Andi flashed a big smile, they both walked to their rooms, to prepare for today's classes.

The end of the day bell rings, Andi yells over to Harper, "meet you at the spot." Harper nodded. The spot was a local bar. Harper arrives before Andi; she grabs their favorite seats, drinks, and food.

Andi comes through the door with the biggest smile on her face. "Hey, are you ready?"

"Ready for what?" Harper replied.

Take out your phone and go to apps. Harper entertained her request; she hands her phone over to Andi. A few taps later Andi hands the phone back to her, with the request "set it up."

Harper looks at what is on her screen, she pushes the phone back with a stern sounding, "NO!" I am not taking no for an answer, let us do this. I have mine set up. It is time to have a little fun. A not too reluctant Harper sets up her Techno page. Techno was the latest dating app, within minutes of her hitting enter, messages started to come in.

In walks, one of their friends into the restaurant they looked at her, saying at the same time, "why are you here?" She replied, "I have met someone on that dumb dating app so I'm meeting him here." Harper, started to ask questions about the app. She wanted to know what type of crazy people she met on this app.

Elise said "that she has not met anyone crazy yet, there's always that fear that you will meet somebody a little off. Just as they start talking about the chance of meeting a strange person."

There was a man standing at the bar waving in their direction. Elise remarks, "that's my date, everyone looked over at the bar," this man was tall well-dressed, handsome did not show signs of being crazy, as she was leaving, we told her to be safe.

Andi and Harper started to talk about their plans, do they really want to use this app? How safe would it be? They made a deal with each other, if they went out on a date, they would let each other know their location.

The fun began, each picked out five pictures for the other. Harper selected Andi's first date, Andi looked at the choices for Harper. She picked Harper's first date and they sent messages to the gentlemen that were selected. Dates were set for later in the week, the ladies made an agreement to meet back at the restaurant Saturday for lunch to talk about how the dates went.

It is Saturday, time for the girls to meet up.

Harper said," Andi we can't sit at the bar to have this conversation. We need a booth away from the crowd."

Andi agreed, they did rock paper scissors to see who would go first, whoever had the worst date had to pay for lunch. Harper won rock paper scissors; she begins with where she met him. It was at one of the local restaurants, they sat in a secluded corner which was strange, but she went along with it. Harper remembered the deal she made with Andi they talked about everything, but nothing personal. They talked about sports, politics, and the weather. As the evening was ending the check came, Harper's date did not reach for the bill, he stood up, thank you he said, he had a fun time and left.

Andi's mouth fell open, she couldn't believe what Harper just told her. She went out on a date, and she had to pay, he didn't offer anything, nor did he stand to pull her chair out. He just walked away. Andi took Harper's phone; she blocked this crazy person. Harper says I told you that they were crazy people this is nothing but a sham, I don't want to deal with this I don't think we should do this anymore but let's hear about your date.

Andi started to tell her about her date, it went well so she felt bad telling Andi how much fun she had, when her date was so horrible. Andi met her date at a park he walked over to the car, opened the door for her. She had packed a picnic lunch for them to eat but when she got there the blanket was out, there were beautiful flowers lying where she was to sit. He had the food set-up, as well as picking out the music, wine, sodas, and water just in case he had the wrong beverage for Andi. They talked about hopes, dreams and where they wanted to be in five years of their lives. Harper was irritated, how did you get the lucky one she said. Is he not creepy? He sounds creepy, he was not, he was short, he came to my shoulder. I don't have anything against short people but that's just not my type of guy, they both burst into laughter,

Harper, remarked, "I want out of this app, I want out of this app now."

Andi replied, "you cannot be out of the app yet, this was just one. You cannot be one and done." This is not some type of drag race where you go down the speed strip at 60,000 miles an hour and just quit, we're not doing that. Out came the pictures again, Harper agreed to one more try at this, so they tried it again, Andi pick for Harper and Harper pick for Andi. OK we're going to meet back here, before we go home, let's reach out to the guys and set our dates and time, then we can see where each other is going. After this date, we can have a conversation about shutting down the app. They both sent messages, the phone started to Ding.

Andi and Harper now have their second dates set. It almost seems like a challenge, or a dare to see who would find the right person first. The ladies will not be able to meet for a few days. Due to the timing of Harper and Andi's dates, it makes it difficult to say when they would see each other. They made a deal not to talk about the dates or the app at work, but their eye contact said something different. Every time one would make a face, the other would burst into laughter. They knew that something was going on and couldn't wait to hang out, to hear what happened. They meet on Saturday at their favorite restaurant, the same bet is in place whoever had the worst date pays for lunch.

When Andi arrives at the restaurant, Harper has 2 shots of tequila waiting for them. Andi looks at her, this isn't going to be a good story I can tell. Ok, I am ready. Harper says no, I went first the last time, you go first. Andi started with her story, she met her date at the bowling alley she noticed that he had gotten her shoes, her bowling ball and snacks for them to nibble on while they were bowling. She noticed he never got up; he stayed seated in the chair. Something's not right, Andi begin to bowl, then she noticed what was wrong. Harper says, what Andi? What did you see? What happened? tell me! tell me!

Andi responds.

"He was a senior citizen that put someone else's photo on the ebsite, to have someone to talk to."

At first Andi was mad, but then she felt sorry for him, so she stayed. She said that was one of the better dates she had in a while. After bowling they went to a movie, it wasn't awkward at all to have his nurse with us. It was good healthy fun. When the night ended, his nurse asked her to wait right there. She walked over to the car, and when she returned, she had two dozen yellow roses. A name brand bag, with all kinds of goodies in it.

Andi said that she could not accept, he responded please, you are a very nice person. I do nice things for nice people. The nurse nodded in agreement; Andi accepted the generous gifts.

Harper orders another round of tequila, she tells Andi while they are getting our order, if you need to go to the restroom, now is the time. She took Harper's advice, she didn't like the look on Harper's face, it made her very concerned.

When Andi returns, she begins to tell the story. Harper walks into this upscale cigar bar. She was wearing a purple dress as agreed upon so that he could find her. It was like in a movie, there he was, a tall, distinguished gentleman, holding a cigar and a shot of bourbon. He begins to walk towards her, he reaches for her elbow to guide her to their table.

The conversation was amazing, they covered everything about each other, yet something was odd. Harper couldn't figure out why Leo was looking over his shoulder throughout the night. She asked if everything was ok, he responded that it was. Sometimes he has clients that come in and interrupt his evening, he just wanted to make sure that didn't happen, since they were having a great time. Not ten minutes after Leo made that statement, he gestured to the bartender to close out the tab.

He said "that he needed to leave because he had an early appointment the next day."

Harper was getting a strange feeling but agreed to end the night early. She noticed two ladies walking towards them with some urgency, Leo grabbed her by the elbow, almost dragging her out the door. Once they got outside, there were 4 women standing there with baseball bats in their hands.

Fear took over Harper's body. The group outside charged Leo, the two women that were inside pushed Harper to the side, she lost her balance fell into the shrubs. Her dress ripped and she lost her shoe.

One of the women helped Harper up, explained that Leo was the lady in the white's husband, and this is where he brings all his Techno dates. The police were called due to the yelling in the parking lot. Leo's wife had beat him almost senselessly and put him into her car. She gave his car keys to one of the ladies, asked her to bring his car home.

Standing there in complete shock, Harper talks to the police, then heads home. She looks up from her tequila at Andi and says I don't think you can top that one. They both sat in silence, Harper says to Andi let's give this a rest. One, I am tired of paying for lunch, and two I am scared that the next time I will not get away from the craziness.

CHAPTER 2

Dating Disappointment

The phone rings,
"Hey are you up?" Andi asks.

"Does it sound like I am up?" Harper replies.

"We have an hour before we need to be in this board meeting, you need to move it!" Andi hangs up the phone.

Harper heads into the shower, "This is going to be a jumpsuit kind of day." Hair in messy ponytail, Harper's breakfast lately, a slice of toast shoved into her mouth, coffee in her hand and down the stairs she goes. Not in the car 5 minutes a message popped up on her phone, Chad.

As Harper was about to click left, she had gone through enough drama. His message was so sweet, she had to respond. Chad wrote, Harper I had to send you a message. Your smile is amazing, your eyes speak to me in ways no other person has on this app.

Harper wonders, is he full of shit? Could he really mean what he says? Could I trust him? After the crazy person that I had gone out with. Do I really want to take a chance on the crazy again? Harper calls Andi, to let her know about the message from Chad. Andi thought it was a sweet note, but not to trust it. Andi also recommended that she continue to talk to the other two guys that were sending messages. Harper took her advice.

She wasn't going to set up another meeting or date until she had longer conversations over text, internet or phone calls. Which made it difficult for Harper, she found three guys that seemed to be nice gentlemen, a quality that Harper wanted in the next person she would go out with. Harper wanted someone who had qualities like her father. It is hard to find a man that opens the door for you, pulls out your chair when you are out eating. Those qualities are so hard to find.

There was a long weekend coming up, Harper made plans to go out of town for the weekend, her trip would take her an hour and a half from Chad. She thought, should I tell him that I am going to be that close to him? Or should I just enjoy my weekend? The closer she got to her destination, she decided to text Chad to let him know that she was going to be in a town close to him.

Chad responded quickly, "he would pack a bag and head that way." Wait what? Harper said to herself, where does he plan to stay? She would worry about that when he arrived. Harper had treated herself to a beautiful suite. The living area had a fireplace that the hotel had going for her when she checked in.

The bedroom was amazingly large, with a jetted tub in the bathroom. The hotel had placed a bottle of champagne next to the tub with roses and candles. This was the nicest thing Harper had treated herself to, since her husband died. With that same thought, a wave of guilt had come over her. Was she wrong for doing this?

Meeting a man at a hotel, with the potential of him staying? Was she ready to possibly sleep with someone? Was she ready to have sex?

"Sex?" no one said anything about sex.

She began to wonder, had she given off signals that she wanted to have sex? Was the information to meet her, while she was on her trip saying she wanted to have sex. Harper started to freak out. Should I let him in? Should I meet him in the lobby to make sure he isn't a serial killer.

'Oh my God!" Harper falls back onto the bed, she yells.

"What in the name of sweet baby Jesus have I done?"

At that moment there was a knock on the door. Harper begins to really freak out.

Should I act like I am not here? Should I let him in?

Harper walks slowly to the door; she keeps the chain on it.

She verifies that it is him, then decides to let him in. He has a suitcase, so let's address this item first. Where do you plan to stay? If you are thinking here, you get the sofa.

As they sit on the sofa, the conversation seems so natural. They are laughing and having a fun time.

Chad "I want to take you out to dinner we can finish our conversation while we eat. then come back, play uno and enjoy this fireplace."

Harper thought to herself this might be a nice date after all.

They got ready to go out, she looked over at Chad, "where are we going for dinner?" He got excited, responded with," Let's go to the Pig Out." Rubbing his hands together like a crazy man in the movies. "I love that place." Harper sat there for a minute, with a dumb look on her face. "This ass is taking me to a drive through." "What a cheap ass".

They are walking to the car; he reaches for her hand to walk through the hallways of the hotel like they are a couple. Harper is still shocked that they are going to a drive through for a dinner date. She says to herself I know that this is not what the dating world is doing now, how cheap. Harper didn't get much, some fries and a milkshake.

Once they returned, they sat on the sofa, he put his hand on her thigh, she felt a feeling that she hadn't felt in a long time. So far, he hadn't shown any signs of being crazy, maybe this will be ok. Harper was longing for the moment that she would feel someone kissing her neck, caressing her body like she was worth more than a hit or miss. As his hand moved up and down her leg, the answer was clear it was time to move into the bedroom.

"Let's go watch TV in the bedroom," she said.

Chad agreed. He turned the fireplace on in the bedroom and turned on the TV. There was a movie on with one of Harper's favorite comedians. She thought to herself, this feels right. She started to fall asleep, then she was feeling a humping on her leg.

With a wrinkled face, the thoughts that were going through her mind were, what is he doing? I am not a tree. It has been 5 years since she has had sex, maybe this is the new way of doing this. With a strong yank of her body, Harper was flat on her back staring at the ceiling with Chad on top of her. OMG! is he going to rape me? What have I done? I can't call Andi, all Harper could do was pray.

Chad looked her in the eyes, he told her how beautiful she was. That he was glad that they were able to meet and spend time with each other. He promised her that she would not forget this night ever. Harper started to relax. Chad started kissing her at the top of her forehead, around the side of her face.

There's that feeling again, but it was stronger. The urge to have someone make love to her, to take her and make her feel whole again. Now he is having slowly made his way to her breast, where he stays there a while, now there is a sense of urgency for this to take place. He continues to take his time with Harper's body. It seems like an episode from a cable show. With her back now arched, the long slow kisses to the inside of her legs are making her entire body shake.

Chad slowly moves his way back to eye contact. Harper says this is it, the moment that she had been waiting for, the last 5 years. His body begins to go in a thrusting motion. He was breathing heavily, calling out Harper's name with every thrust. But wait, shouldn't I feel anything? Harper was thinking. Shouldn't there be a warm sensation inside of me? Then the speed picks up, Chad begins to make strange noises, then a yell for Jesus, he rolls over. He had completed his mission, while Harper is still laying there looking at the ceiling asking herself was that it?

What is that noise? Chad was snoring, she grabbed her phone slipped into the bathroom to text Andi. YOU WILL NOT BELIEVE WHAT JUST HAPPENED. The LOL! Emoji's she sent to Harper didn't stop until they were at least 20 deep. She suggested that Harper leave, but it's her hotel room. She had to stay. Throughout the night Andi kept sending text messages, you were so close LOL. Harper woke him up around 5:00am and told him he had to leave, because she was heading home at 6:00am. Which was far from the truth, she was staying an extra day. She needed it after what just happened. She went shopping to take her mind off that mess.

As soon as Harper returned home, she told Andi to remove this app. She is not dealing with this crap anymore. I got people who want me to pay the tab, men getting beat up because they are on a dating app. This time a man who thinks he is having sex with you but really jabbing the mattress. Just make the app go away.

Andi never listens to one thing Harper says. Andi says before we delete the app, let me try one thing. She has one last ditch effort, to see if she can make this work for Harper. Andi updates Harper's profile with new pictures and changes the location. Andi promises Harper that in two weeks if nothing happens, they will be done. A week has gone by and nothing new has come from the app. Andi and Harper goes to the bar, the weather is good, they grab a seat outside with chips and salsa, tequila, the ladies are having a good time enjoying the band

Harper's phone beeps, she looks at the phone, then she looks at Andi. Before Harper could look at the phone again, Andi took the phone away. She opens the message, there was a 6 foot four athletic built gentleman responding to Harper's photos. He had eyes that could see through your soul. Harper tried to get her phone back but Andi kept it.

Andi said " I'm going to respond this time," she hit the reply button with a simple hello. Before Andi could put the phone down he responded, "I love your smile and your eyes. Andi replies your eyes are amazing would you like to talk more?

The phone Rings with one word reply yes, they both giggled like 2 little high school girls that had just saw the new kid in school.

Andi still holding Harper's phone says when would you like to meet? The phone went silent.

Harper said, "see I told you this was not going to work."

We got excited for nothing, the phone beeped. His reply was, I would like to get to know you through the app first and then let's meet, Andi replies that's cool.

Over the next few weeks, every morning there was a text simply saying, good morning, how are you doing, how was your day? This went on for weeks as they got to know each other or so they thought they were getting to know each other. One morning a different message comes through, it says would you like to meet?

Harper looks at her phone, she has a big grin on her face, she looks at her phone again. It took an hour before she responded. When she does, she says what date works for you? Justice responds how about next Wednesday? Without hesitation, Harper says yes, is 6:00 o'clock, ok? He says yes, where would you like to go? How about that Italian restaurant Olivia's greenhouse? Ok! It's a date, says Justice.

Harper couldn't wait to get to work to tell Andi about what happened. She says that she got a message that says hey Are you ready to meet and she responded yes, they set the date up. Now we are a week away from meeting him. Harper wasn't nervous until Andi started asking questions. What are you going to wear? What are you going to eat? If you eat pasta, you can't eat spaghetti, don't drink red wine in case you spill it. How are you going to wear your hair? What shoes are you going to wear? Harper's nerves had started to kick in. She was having nerves like she had never had on any of the other dates. She just looked at Andi with a blank stare, I have no idea.

Wednesday is here, Harper left work early to get ready. Hair up in a messy ponytail, white jeans, a form fitting top, and flat sandals, she is ready to go. Before she heads out, Harper looks in the mirror, this will have to do. I don't know what else to wear, I don't want to seem like I am desperate, or give off anymore sex signals.

Harper arrives one hour early to get a seat, if she needs to run, she can. She sits near the door, she changes her mind, asked the waitress could she move closer to the bar? Harper can see the parking lot, as he walks into the building. Knowing she would be an hour early, she brought work with her. She had schedules to get together, work, trips, family vacations, that she needed to get into her planner. While she was working on her planner, her phone rang. It was Justice, I'm in the parking lot he says.

Harper's heart started beating fast, she didn't know what to do. Should she leave, or should she stay? There's no turning back, do not think about the bad experience that you had in the hotel room. Let that go, start over, this is something different. Don't compare this to the past dates, you will ruin it before it starts. She sent him a text to let him know where she was sitting.

She thought she saw him walking into the building but she wasn't sure, there was someone who looked like his photo walking towards the table. He was tall, with an athletic build, his eyes, oh Lord his eyes, she stood up to greet him. They greeted with a hug, a shiver came over her body, unlike the one she had at the hotel, which was a disaster, stop thinking about that she said to herself, this is not the same.

Justice ordered a drink, Harper ordered round two for herself. The conversation was great, they talked about family, friends, and their jobs. The food came, Harper took Andi's advice, she did not order spaghetti she ordered lasagna and a salad, something that she could eat with a fork. The food was good, the conversation was better, the laughs were endless. This was comfortable to her, he reached for her hand across the table, he held her hands through the entire conversation.

The sun that was shining bright when they both came into the restaurant is now a shining moon. The restaurant that once was full of people, now only the two of them are left and they were being asked to leave by the restaurant's owner. Harper gathered her things, she picked up the check, and walked to the register. She paused for a moment, wait this was a date. It's not the same as the dates before. Harper was the one who picked up the check, she continued to the register to pay. Justice waited outside to hold the door for her. They walked towards Harper's car, to find out they had parked next to each other.

Harper leaning on her car, Justice leaning on his. This is an awkward moment, Harper thought. She says to herself do I kiss him? Do I hug him? Or should I shake his hand? She didn't have to answer that, Justice answered it for her. He grabbed her by the small of her waist and pulled her close to him.

There was that shiver again, the one you get when your high school crush is near or when they bump into you at the lockers. Harper, not knowing if she should kiss him, hug him, or walk away, she put her head into his chest.

He takes both hands, places them on her cheeks, lifts her face to where he can see her eyes. He kissed her forehead, then moved to her nose. At this point, Harper could feel more than shivers, she takes a step back, even though she really wants to stay.

Then it happens he begins to kiss her like she has not been kissed before or since college, she knows, she should pull back, but the attraction was too strong. When the long passionate kiss was complete, she wasn't sure what she should do next.

Once Harper catches her breath and realizes what happened, without a thought she leans back into his chest. The parking lot emptied during the 30 minutes of nonstop kissing. This must stop, before sexual acts happen. Harper pulls away, she says, it is time for her to go home. He pulls her back into his arms. One more kiss, he asks, she leans in to give him another kiss, a flash of lightning appears with the one last kiss, they both agreed to see each other the following Sunday.

Justice asked Harper, "What would you like to do, she says, "I like walking along the riverbank, anything with water will be ok. Picnics in the park are great, he says, you pick something and let me know. One last time, Justice leans in for a kiss. Harper heads home, she stops at a gas station to fill her tank up. Her phone rings, she looks at the message,

"I had a wonderful time."

her response, "I did too, I wish I could have stayed longer."

Justice responds, "come back to me,"

Harper wished she could, but she had to be at work at 8:00 in the morning, it was almost midnight now and she needed to go home. Once she was home, the first thing she did was call Andi, she put her on speakerphone she told her everything that had happened. Andi was screaming in the phone, oh my God Oh my God this is the one this is the one. I'm excited for you, when you get to work tomorrow, we will have lunch together and we will discuss the details of what you are going to do on Sunday.

Harper and Andi made a deal that they would never discuss techno at work, any techno conversations were to be had outside of the workplace. When they had a lunchbreak, they would have to go outside the building, to keep their promise to each other even if it meant sitting in a car just to talk about. Harper and Andi while in the car, they laughed and giggled like two little high school students who had just gone out on their very first date, it was a first date for Harper. Now what do I do about Sunday?

Andi says wear something cute and just be yourself. Harper is wearing jean shorts, a tank top, she checked the mirror, out the door she went. When she arrived at the address she was given, it was an empty parking lot. Harper put the address in the GPS one more time to make sure she was right. The address he gave Harper was getting her lost. She sent him a message, "you gave me the wrong address."

he says "I gave you the right address I am sure, where are you?

At first Harper was a little taken back by his tone, when he found her, she was only three blocks away. His facial expression didn't match the tone on the phone, so she continued to follow him to his house. Once she got there, he said give me a few minutes to get everything together, we'll hop back in my car, and start our date. This was fine with Harper, it is Sunday, and a beautiful day outside, we have all day. While he was getting things together, there was a football game on the TV she stopped to watch.

He was shocked, even though she told him that she likes sports, Justice was happy to see that she watches football, she also, knows what was going on. He played college football, he told Harper, to date someone he says, who knows sports, was important for him. She thought about what he said for a minute to "date someone." This is the second time we've met so we aren't dating so let's just not say that. They continued to watch the game; she was tucked under his arm with him rubbing her shoulder.

Harper jumped up; she began to yell at the TV about a bad call. Justice let out a big laugh because he didn't believe that she was that into sports. Ok, let's get ready to go, can I use your restroom please? Sure, no problem he replied. When Harper came out of the restroom, Justice grabbed her by her waist, pulled her so close to him that she couldn't breathe. He told her that he had waited all week to do this again.

The kiss was unlike the one in the parking lot, there was passion, attraction that was undeniable. He was now holding both sides of her face, she also could tell that there was more than kissing on his mind without saying anything. This was not what I had planned, Harper said to herself. It was like she was frozen or having an out of body experience that she was watching unfold.

His hands went from her face, slowly down her shoulders as his lips slowly kissed behind her ear, down her neck to the center of her breast. His hands stopped at her waist, he pulled her shirt off and threw it on the floor. Not sure who had taken over her body, she took off his shirt, then she unbuckled his pants.

Justice grabbed her by the hand and led her into his bedroom, everything happens with such urgency. As he slowly made his way back to eye contact level, Harper let out a slight Oh! He asked what's wrong? Nothing. Harper wasn't going to compare the two, but DAM! Will I be able to walk when this is over? I don't care, this is one thing that I have been missing and if this is to be the last time for a while again, I will enjoy it.

Harper did things that she had never done during marriage. For the duration of her marriage, it was the same day and the same way. Being with Justice, you could be yourself without judgement. Sex is meant to be enjoyed not regulated. A few hours later, with messed up hair, and exhausted, it was time for her to go.

They never got a chance to go out as planned. Harper goes to the bathroom to clean up, Justice is standing outside of the bathroom, with a soda and apologies for what happened. She told him that there was no need for that. She was as willing as he was. In the back of her mind, she thought now that they have had sex, he will ditch her. Isn't that what most of them do on this dating app. Hit it and quit it?

CHAPTER 3

Is he the one?

I want to see you again, when is your next free date? She asked if he picked the dates since he works in the afternoon, this would be easier for him to find the dates. They started to see each other 3 times a week for a couple of months. There was something in the back of Harper's mind that she couldn't let go, this was not a relationship so no need to rock the boat. She had to tell Andi what she was feeling.

Andi came over to her house, tell me if I am crazy or not. We have been going out for about two months now, I have yet to meet any of his friends. Also, he only hangs around females. There is one that he spends a lot of time with, when I asked about her, he says she is just like one of the boys and I was reading too much into it. A frown came over Andi's face, what's wrong? I agree with you, this doesn't sound right.

Harper pulls up his social media page, look, this is what I am talking about. I am reading too much into this. Andi says cut back a little bit to see what happens. Harper goes from 3 days to one.

Justice reactions was, ok I understand if you are busy. This didn't sit well with her at all. They had tickets for a two-day concert, so she stopped by his apartment. He was still at work; he would meet her down there in a few hours.

No text no show. Harper was going to pack her bags and return home. There was a knock on the door, it was Justice. He could tell she was mad, he gave her flowers, again with sorry. He took her out for a lovely seafood dinner. They got dressed for the concert, he said he needed to step outside for a moment, he would meet her at his truck.

What's going on? He is like Jekyll and Hyde. When she got to the truck he was in a good mood and ready to go. This was a two-day concert so what are they going to do all day tomorrow? They will talk about it in the morning. They had a great time, Justice was taking photos, it was an amazing night.

Morning comes, Harper is getting up to get dressed to go out for breakfast. Justice is getting dressed also, not for breakfast, but to return home. What the hell is this? I have a job to do, I will be back before the concert . We can have dinner when I return, you pick the place, just leave Harper says.

Justice didn't blink, he grabbed his bag and left. His clients are more important than the weekend we have planned. At that very moment, she thought about calling someone, anyone, to come pick her up. She goes to her happy place, the beach. When Harper gets angry, the 1ˢᵗ place she goes to is the beach. As she sat in the sand staring out at the water, she was asking herself, why would he leave? He knew that we had this entire weekend planned. I do not care if it is an hour away, you just do not leave.

He returned five hours later; you could cut the tension in the room with a knife. They got dressed, to head to the concert. Harper could not wait for this weekend to be over. She was so upset with his actions. When they returned to the hotel, Justice jumped into the shower. He told Harper that he had something special for her. She smiled; I have something special for you also.

While Justice was in the shower, Harper grabbed her bags that she had packed before heading to the beach. She slowly opened the door, pushed one bag out the door then the other. Justice is in the shower singing to the top of his lungs. The door closed behind her gently. She stopped by the front desk to let them know that the man in the room was paying the bill, gave them his license plate number. She was gone, not 20 minutes after she left, he texted "where are you at".

She replied, "wait there, in the outfit I love to see you in, I will be right back." She is 30 minutes from her house, her phone rings, she refuses to pick it up. Then he starts to text her. "All your shit is gone. I know you didn't leave me here alone. That's some messed up shit!!!" No more than what you did to me. "How many times do I have to tell you that I do not have a 9-5 job like you do. Some of the jobs are easier on the weekends with no one in the building. I also had to teach a class. You know what I do for a living."

Two weeks have gone by, no word from Justice. Harper and Andi are at work trying to get students' schedules together for the following school year. The conference room door opens, a co-worker sticks her head in, Harper you have a visitor. Not sure who could be in the lobby, Harper heads towards the lobby. There he stood 6'4" holding flowers with a smile and those eyes that could make you say yes to a sandstorm home.

She walks towards him, with 6 feet between them, he starts, I am sorry. Harper in returns ask, "Sorry for what?" Justice replies, I am sorry for making you feel that you are not important. I am sorry for leaving you alone when the weekend was supposed to be about us. Can we start over? Everything in her body was telling her to run. It was like a magnet; she was pulled into his arms. Flowers fell to the floor; he began to kiss her like no one was around.

Andi comes out of the conference room, yells at Harper to come back into the meeting. Embarrassed by her actions, she kissed Justice goodbye. He told her that he would be waiting for her when she got off from work. Andi, standing in the room with her hands on her hips, and right foot tapping the floor.

"What the hell was that?"

"Um a kiss?" Harper replies.

"I don't need your smart-ass answers" "I need to know what you are thinking?" Andi responds.

"He said he was sorry!"

"So that makes everything ok? Says Andi.

"Yes!" Harper replies.

The room went quiet for what seemed like hours, it was only 5 minutes. Andi extended her arms to Harper; she gave her a big hug. "All I want you to know, that no matter what happens I will always be here for you." With tears in her eyes, Harper looked at Andi and thanked her for her friendship.

Things could not have been going better in Harper's eyes. She was learning to except the photos that he would post on the social media sites with the other females. She eventually began to put it out of her mind that she had yet to meet his mother, sisters and children. His reason was that he had just gone through a bad break-up with his fiancé and did not want to bring someone else into their lives until he knew this one was going to last. This sounds logical to her.

It had been a long time since Harper had a large birthday party; this was the year. She was planning an old fashion backyard cookout style birthday. Since it was being held at a park, Harper had no limits on how many people she could invite. Also, this would be a fun time for everyone to meet Justice. As the planning for her party continued, Harper wanted to take a trip out of the country just to relax and enjoy some time away from everything.

As she was planning the trip, she learned that Justice didn't have a passport, so they had to travel to places that didn't require a passport. Here's she is planning a trip for the two of them to go away, everything is booked. She has paid for both. One week away from the trip, Justice says he doesn't think he will be able to go.

"What the hell?" she yells into the phone.

"I don't think that I can leave my business that long" he replied.

Harper is now in a full-blown yell into the phone, if you don't go you owe me $1,500, it got quiet.

"I will see what I can do to make this work". Said Justice.

It's Sunday, Harper has arrived at his house. Justice was in a bad mood. You could tell that he didn't want to go. Reluctantly he put his bag into the car, and they went to the airport. While waiting for the plane, Justice received a call. He turned to Harper to ask the details of the trip, what day they were coming back. When she answered, he kicked his luggage and walked away.

He was gone for at least 20 minutes, and when he returned, he was a different person. Feeling uneasy about what was going on, she asked if everything was, ok? He responded of course why would you ask? You kicked your luggage and walked away pissed off when I told you the date. I was pissed off, I had no clue that we were going to be gone this long. I have a job that I needed to do, I was able to get things moved to the day after we returned, all is good.

Still not feeling comfortable about what just took place, Harper settled back to enjoy herself. She has her birthday party planned for next month, no need to focus on that while on her trip. She is ready to spend time with this man she is trying hard not to fall for. After a long 5-hour flight, they have arrived in St. Thomas. This is a beautiful place; the water was so clear you could see the sand beneath your feet. Harper unpacked her bag, changed into a swimsuit to head out to the beach. He was frantically looking to see how he could connect to the internet.

Not being able to connect at that moment, that side came out of him that Harper was not happy to see and sometimes scared of, so she left the room. Walking to the beach, she thought about stopping at the front desk, to get the information needed. She changed her mind and continued to the beach. A few hours went by, before Justice joined her at the beach, once again he acted like nothing was wrong.

Harper was thinking to herself, she is not sure how much longer she will be able to put up with the mood swings. For now, they are far away from everything and everyone, this would be a fun time to grow closer or just find out what type of person he really is. 30 minutes into his arrival at the beach, he had not said a word. Harper rises from the chair to sit in the water, she looks back to see if he was heading to join her, the entire time he was on his phone.

All she could think about was taking a photo with him, so that she would have a picture like all the others. She got out of the water and headed towards Justice. He was walking in her direction. A smile came over her , at that moment the vacation started. He began to pay attention to her, they were taking photos, going out to dinner and seeing the sights. Not once did she see the crazy person she had seen at the start of the trip.

The mini vacation is coming to an end. Harper spoke too soon; Jekyll and Hyde were starting to show when they arrived at the airport. Justice began to get an unrest about himself, he couldn't sit still and was getting upset that the plane was taking too long to get there. Again, Harper has that uneasy feeling about being around him.

"Was he scared of flying?" Harper thought to herself.

"Was he in a rush to return home?" What could this craziness be?

Harper pulled out her phone to text Andi, she wanted to give her an update on what the trip was like, how he was acting and that she was a bit scared. In Andi's text, once you land and return home safely, I really want you to get away from him. There is something not right and I can't put my finger on it. Harper reluctantly agreed, she stayed quiet the rest of the trip.

Once safely back at the airport, she was heading towards her car, Justice grabbed her arm. Fear flew into Harper, not knowing what he was going to do. He pulled her close to him holding her by the waist, thanking her for one of the best trips he ever had?

"What? Was he on the same trip as I was?" Harper thought to herself.

She stuttered, "you are welcome, I am glad you had a good time."

"I had an amazing time, any time spent with you is an enjoyable time." Yes, he's crazy, Andi is right I need to get away from this as fast as possible. I will see you at your birthday party sounds like it's going to be a good time. "Wait, what? My birthday party, which is a month away. So, you are not going to see me for another month?" was Harper's response.

"Oh no. that's not what I was saying. I am just saying that I am looking forward to spending time with you again next month."

"Um, ok sure." Harper gave him a good-bye kiss and started her drive home. The drive from the airport to her house was about an hour, the same distance to Justice's house. During this drive she thought about everything that Andi had said. All the crazy things that Justice had done on the trip and before the trip.

She began to list the things that were not right. She was saying them aloud.

1. I have never met his family, mom, sister, daughter or son.
2. I have never met his friends. The so-called "just buddies."
3. He has never posted photos of me and himself on his social media.

4. We never go out to public places where he lives.

5. He always has an excuse why he can't make major holidays with me and my family, yet he posts photos of him and his "buddies", when we should be together.

6. There was never an impulsive trip, everything had to be planned.

7. I have now gone from 3 times a week visits to just Sunday's.

Harper shook her head, there's got to be something good about this relationship. It took her some time to think of at least 3 things.

1. Was it sex? Why is that the first thing I come up with? Harper says. It is good though. It's truly the best I have had since college. She chuckles to herself; I know someone would say what about your husband? He was predictable, she thought. He had set days and times, same position. With Justice she was free to be who she wanted to be with no judgement.

2. We talk about sports; we both love football and basketball.

3. He's stupid and he makes me laugh.

Harper continues to drive, "Is that it? My cons far outweigh my pros!" There are so many red flags. What do I do now? She could hear Andi's voice, saying leave his ass that's what you do.

She finally arrives home; her phone rings, are you home yet? Andi asked. "Yes, I am here." response Harper. I am on the way. Within 15 minutes, the door opens, Andi marches directly to her.

Give me your phone, give it to me now. Harper looks puzzled why do you want my phone. I am removing and blocking Justice. Harper with a stern look on her face reply's "the hell you preach!"

You need to be rid of this person, he's no good for you. I told you that I would always have your back. I don't want to delete him just yet. Let me share my thoughts with you while I was driving home. I have concluded that I am with him for the sex. Which by the way is not that bad. Andi continues to listen. I know that I need to leave but my plan is to stay with him and use him for the sex until something better comes along. If he's using me then let me have a little bit of that action.

Reluctant to agree with Harper, Andi promised that she would hold off on sharing her thoughts, but if he hurt her, there would be hell to pay. So, they began to go over the plans for her birthday party. This party has now gotten to 50 plus people coming including Justice. Andi asked how are you going to introduce him. That's a good question, I will keep him as a Plus one. Never a boyfriend will he be.

CHAPTER 4

Birthday Party

The much-awaited birthday party is finally here. Andi and Harper's childhood friend Elise has flown in from Dubai for the party. In addition to the party, Elise has plans to meet this person who has entered Harper's life. This party was like a high school reunion, all Harper's high school classmates, co-workers and family were in attendance. This was the party that she always wanted to happen.

There was dancing, card games, board games, all kinds of fun things to do. Her cousin was cooking an old-fashioned fish fry, it was perfect. Harper looked out of the corner of her eye, and there he was, walking into the cookout. Everyone slowly started to stare, it wasn't that he was the finest man in the park. It was because he was wearing a bright yellow cartoon shirt with matching shoes.

Harper didn't care, she was so excited that he came to the event. In her heart she didn't think he would show up. His past actions wouldn't support that he would come. They greeted each other with a hug and a kiss. She could feel people staring, again she didn't care. When she turned around, Andi and Elise were standing there.

"Ok, we have waited long enough!" "Who is this?" Elise said.

"I am Justice" with his hand extended.

With serious hesitation, she shook it. I am Andi, you don't have to introduce yourself to me. I have heard enough about you to know who you are. Harper gave her a look.

Then she softens it a little bit, before you walk around with Harper to meet her family and friends, can we sit down and chat a little bit? Justice didn't want any parts of this, and you could see that side of him starting to come out.

Harper grabbed him and told them they could talk to him later. I am going to let him meet other people and eat. After meeting people she brought the introduction to an end. They played a game of Jenga, with the crowd watching. There was a lot of trash talking between Justice and Harper, the smile that was on both of their faces was a sign to all that there was something between the two.

After Harper won two games, Justice got a plate of food and Harper returned to talking to others at the party, and that's when Andi and Elise took the opportunity to hit him with a ton of questions.

"Do you care about Harper?"

"Why can't she meet your family?"

"Why are you hiding her?"

"We know you care, because you are here, but what do you really want from her?"

Harper gets a tap on her shoulder; Justice says he got a call and needs to return home.

"Happy birthday, I will talk to you at a later time."

You could see the tears building up in her eyes. She walked with him back to his car. She asked if everything was, ok? When he turned to look at her, it was like he hated her, his voice changed he replied,

"Everything is FINE!"

"I have no idea what lies you have told your friends. But you need to step back and look at this." You and your friends are reading more into this than it is. I am out.

He sped off, while Harper stood in the parking space watching him leave. She started to cry uncontrollably, one of her high school friends came over, "you can do better than that." Harper lost it, don't tell me what is best for me. You don't know him and don't compare him to my dead husband. They are two different people.

By the time Harper got back down the hill to where her party was happening, there was someone at every turn, saying that she could do better. Where did you meet him at? He doesn't look like someone you should be around. To stop the tears, and anything else that would come out of her mouth, Harper started drinking and dancing.

All she wanted to do was masked the pain that she was feeling. The party was ending, guests were leaving, some with hugs and good wishes. The others with I am sorry I hope your party wasn't ruined. One guest pulled Harper to the side to talk.

Have a seat she took a deep breath. Harper, I understand the things that was said to you tonight was not a good feeling. I believe that they all meant well, when they said you can do better. I watched the two of you together and could see that you were happy. Yes, I think that they all were comparing him to your late husband and that is not fair. They also didn't take the time to get to know him.

All I want to say is to follow your heart and listen to your brain. They battle each other sometimes, if you stay strong you will find what you are looking for. As soon as Harper got home, she called Justice, and they talked about what happened at the party. She would not apologize for her friends, but explained he was the first person that she had brought around the group since her husband had died. Instead of them accepting you for who you are, they started to compare you to my late husband.

They both agreed to put this behind them and continue with their situation ship. They also agreed that they were friends, who enjoyed each other's time and hanging out. Now that a clear definition of the relationship or the lack thereof, Harper and Justice are now in a good place.

To make sure that the lines would never get blurred, Harper reached out to Leo, he still wanted to see her. He didn't care that she was seeing Justice, Leo would continue to reach out to her, check in on her to make sure she was doing ok. Also, to remind her that he would be there for her when this relationship fails.

CHAPTER 5

Let Him go!

Andi and Harper had been working hard trying to meet school deadlines. Harper realized that she hadn't talked to Justice in two weeks. She turned to Andi "it's been two weeks since I have talked to him,"

she responds to Harper.

"If you made it this long then you need to keep it that way."

Harper looked down at the ground, in a quiet voice said, "you are right."

Harper's phone buzzes with a number that she had never seen. She looks at it, there's a message on there.

"I am glad you have come to your senses and stopped seeing Justice! He is seeing Kourtney; they are a couple now, nothing you can do or say will break them up!"

She threw the phone across the room; Andi picked it up to read the message and both were upset. Harper sent Justice a screenshot of what she got, along with the photos that came with it. He got an attitude with her saying he doesn't recognize the number and wasn't dealing with her crazy shit.

Hurt and crying, Harper didn't say anything else to him about the messages, photo or his attitude. She kept her Sunday visits, but every visit was strained and awkward. While they were watching TV her phone beeped, there was another incoming message. She handed the phone to Justice, he was pissed.

He responded to the message.

"I just want you to know that Justice is here with Kourtney, he went into the house as I was leaving. I hope you will finally leave him alone."

"How did you see me leave anywhere when I am here with the person that you are texting. I hope for your sake that I never find out who this is." Justice ended the message handed Harper her phone, apologized that this was happening to her.

The phone beeps again, Justice takes it from her. "Why are you sending messages back acting like you are Justice, that's not going to work with me. I am smarter than that."

Justice hops up, grabs his keys, tells Harper to stay here he would be right back. She was puzzled but agreed that she would stay there. He also asked her to keep responding to the text messages. Until he sent her a text.

"What the hell are you doing Justice?" Harper yells out the door.

"I am going to make this shit stop once and for all" he yells back.

As asked, Harper continued the messages for 20 minutes, they went back and forth, somewhere mean, some of them had photos of Justice and Kourtney. The last one was very scary.

"This is your last message; I am tired of this back-and-forth shit. I have told you that they are a couple, he will never want you, and if you don't leave, we can't say what will happen to you"?

Harper was afraid to respond to that one, then her phone beeped again. With a message that made her heart drop.

"Hey Babe, its Justice, you will not have to worry about getting anymore messages, I know who is sending them. I will be home in a few minutes."

An hour later Justice comes through the door with dinner, flowers and the phone that was being used to send messages to her. Justice started off with an apology, for the way he treated her, for not believing that she was sending the messages to herself. While he was driving back, he realized that he needed to spend more time with her to get things back on track.

"I know that you and Andi are on a big deadline, once you finish can I take you to the beach?" "I know that is your favorite place to go, to unwind and relax. Let's do that together?"

Harper wanted to believe that he meant what he was saying that he really wanted to spend time with her. She wasn't sure that he wanted to make amends with her. Or was it because he now doesn't have his partner-in-crime to hang out with?

As she stood up to leave, he grabbed her by the waist and pulled her close to him. Looked her in the eyes, and vowed he would never hurt her again. He would not let anyone hurt her or what they are working on. At that moment, she realized that she loved this man and would be willing to work through the problems that they have.

Before she realized it, Justice had picked her up, with her arms wrapped around his neck, he walked back to the bedroom. Gently placing her on the bed, he began to kiss her starting at the top of her head. Just a soft peck down the side of her face, down her neck to the center of her breast. Harper wanted him to stop, she wanted to talk about what had just happened. The more he kissed her the less she wanted to talk to him.

She closed her eyes, he whispered in her ear, "relax don't do anything, I want to show you how much I love you and how sorry that I am for everything." Music started to play; one by one, her clothes slowly started to come off. Her mind was clearly saying "leave." She could not, her body was craving something that she felt only he could give her.

Harper relaxed, Justice made love to her, like he has never had in the time that they have been together. Repeatedly he said that he loved her. When this marathon sex session started, the sun was up. They had gone 4 hours wrapped up in each other, that the events of the day seem so long ago. Harper stayed the night, and the sex continued throughout the night, she calls work the next morning to let them know she would be in at noon.

Andi and Elise texted her asking if she was, ok? If they needed to come pick her up, what was going on? She responded I can't walk, not giving her a chance to say why. They asked her to drop a pin for her location they were coming to get her. Harper fell back on the bed in laughter, she responded in 5 words. "He Put It on Me! He told me he loved me!"

No response after that, then 20 minutes later, "meet us at the bar after work!" Harper responding "NOPE! If you are going to lecture me about this and tell me what I should or shouldn't do, I respectfully decline."

The next few weeks, the girls really didn't say anything about Justice to her. Harper and Andi both got promotions for the project they completed; it was time for them to celebrate. Champagne is flowing, laughter and cheers all around. Andi goes over to Harper to give her a hug, "remember I will always have your back!" I know you will, you always do Andi, I don't want this to come between us. Andi "it won't."

Let's make a deal, when you two come back from the beach next week. I will start going to his classes with you, I want to show support for both of you. I am happy that he has started to invite you to his classes. When did he do that? The same day he found out who was sending the text messages. "What? Wait, who was sending the messages to you?"

"Do you remember, his bestie that is always in the photos and classes with him? They called themselves, Ike and Tina?" Harper says.

Andi replies, "yes."

"It was her!" she says.

At that moment, Andi begins to cuss, she threw her hands up in the air at the statement, she forgot that she had a drink in her hand. The alcohol spilled all over one of the customers, he stood up and it was Chad. Harper never saw him sitting in there, why was he here? Andi apologized repeatedly. Then she stopped," wait, you two know each other?"

Yes, this is Chad we had breakfast last year, Harper turns to him to see why he is in her town. His response, that he had a job to do, brought him to her town. All of this is by chance that you would show up in a place that I had stopped to eat on my way home. I was not prepared to get covered in champagne. I am going to go across the street to grab a dry shirt and pants. Will you two stay for a little bit, I will treat you both to dinner and another round of drinks.

Harper was about to say no, when Andi says sure, we will be here, take your time. Once he is out of sight, Andi looks at Harper he's cute. No, let's not start, he's short! Did you just say that he was short? Yes, I did say he was short. I have nothing against short guys, they are not for me. Andi gave her a funny look, part confused and part disappointed. Chad returned in fresh clothes, they all sat down and had a great afternoon.

Harper saw a side of Chad that she had not seen before, she liked what she saw. For the 1st time she didn't see his height she saw the person that he was. The three of them were in the restaurant until it closed. Since it was late, out of kindness Harper offered Chad her sofa so he wouldn't have to drive back home with alcohol in his system and it being late.

They called a ride-share for Andi, her safety was just as important to Harper as Chad's. Once they got to Harper's house, they sat and talked until the sun came up. It was so refreshing to talk to someone who cared about things that you liked. Harper told Chad that she had always wanted to write a book. The reason she hadn't, her family and friends thought she was wasting her time.

He told her that it will happen when the passion outweighs the doubt. There will be a topic that will move her to write and nothing anyone will say will stop the passion. Harper, feeling very sleepy, got up to shower and prepare for work. Chad was off for the day, she told him that he could stay at her house to rest. She would take him to pick his car up when she returned.

It was an exceptionally long day for Harper and Andi, both tired and hung over, they pushed through the day with the help of a lot of coffee and energy drinks. As the day closed Andi asked Harper if she could drop her off to pick her car up. I must drop off Chad so I can take you both at the same time.

The ladies entered Harper's home and there was an amazing smell. When they reached the second floor, there was a beautiful table set for two. For a moment he was startled to see Andi, coming up the stairs behind her.

"Hello Andi" Chad said, "Let me grab another plate and silverware."

Andi was quick to say "no, I am not staying."

Chad responded "I insist please there's plenty, we can pick up our conversation from last night. I had a fun time getting to know you both."

As Chad sat the table for an added person, the two ladies were hitting each other, like two kids in high school. When he turned around to see them laughing, his remark was I don't even want to know what's going on with you two. Holding glasses of wine, he invited the ladies to take a seat. He began to serve an Italian dinner, salad, pasta, bread and a chocolate dessert that was better than a restaurant. While enjoying the meal both wondered, where did you get the items to cook with.

Chad "It's new technology, called window dash." Everyone began to laugh, with remarks coming from both ladies calling him a smart-ass. Harper's phone had been beeping non-stop during dinner. It was Justice, asking her where she was, why she hadn't returned his calls. Was she upset about what happened a few days ago? She excused herself for a moment to respond to the text. "I am unavailable now. I will text you as soon as I am free." She returned to the table without her phone, and the three continued to have fun. Harper was taking everyone back to get their cars, they all agreed they needed to do this again.

Now home alone, she reached out to Justice, I am home now what would you like to talk about? We need to start spending more time together like we did in the beginning. I didn't see that any of my friends would do something like that to you. "Friend? She was more than a friend." Harper responded. "You are correct, she was like my best friend." Justice continued "when are you coming to see me?" There was a long pause, then Harper responded, "I will continue to keep my Sunday, until things turn around for us."

I understand and respect your stand on it. Does this mean that you and your friend are not going to take my class? Harper's response was quick, "yes we will be there for the class, the only day that I will spend the night with you will be Sunday." He accepted her response, he looked forward to seeing her on Wednesday. Still not comfortable going to a class that his friends are attending, Harper looked for the cutest outfit she could find.

On the drive down to Justice's class, the ladies sang to the top of their lungs. They arrived at the workout location, they didn't see his car in the parking lot, they looked at each other, both wondering what they should do. After a few minutes, they both grabbed their bags, went into the building and found a spot to set up to shake off the nerves.

While setting up Harper, she sees one of Justice's work out friends, she goes over to say hello and that she enjoyed watching the workouts online. Her name was Dina. She was giving off a strange vibe, Harper continued to talk to her when Justice walks through the door, he sees them talking. He stopped in his tracks when both spoke to him in that loving voice that you would use with your boyfriend. Harper ignored this, when she probably shouldn't have. She walked over to Justice and gave him a hug, with the hug that was tight and meaningful he said in her ear that he was glad that she was there.

When he let her go, he walked over to Andi, the two of them were acting silly. While this was going on Harper glanced over at Dina, who seemed to have a very mean look on her face. Once his attention was no longer on us and back on teaching the class, Dina became loud, and the center of attention. The louder she was the more attention that was paid to her. After class was over, Justice always takes photos, Andi and Harper stayed out of them. The group was calling for them to get into the photos. Why not, the only person that is getting upset with it was Dina.

On the ride back home, the ladies talked about how much fun they had, both talked about how strange Dina was acting. There was one lady there they both liked, her name was Lyssa. She had a lot of energy and made the work out fun. Cannot wait to see her again,

Harper looked at Andi, "are you going back with me next week?" Oh, course she responded.

If there is nothing going on or I have a date, I will be there. For the next month they were regulars every Wednesday. Andi started to see someone on a regular basis, his only day off from work was Wednesday. Harper told Andi how happy she was for her, she encouraged Andi to find the love she deserves.

It is time to go to class, Harper is packed and ready to go. When she arrives, the only people that are in the building were Dina and Harper. You could cut the tension with a knife, Dina asked if she knew that Justice's birthday was in a few weeks. She replied that she did, Dina continues to share that she would like to have something special for him since his birthday falls on a Saturday. He would be teaching class so to surprise him with breakfast would be nice.

Harper asked what she could do to help. Dina gave her a list of things that she could pick up, bagels, fresh cut fruit, sandwiches, orange juice and cake. Harper looked at her and asked, "what are you bringing? Dina had the lunch side of things; she just needed the breakfast covered. Harper hesitated, she agreed to the request.

She took the class; it didn't have the same energy as it had in past classes. She grabbed her stuff, left out of the building. No photos, no good-byes, nothing.

Harper thought that when she arrived home, she would have a text asking if everything was ok. There was nothing, she took a shower to prepare for bed. When she finally relaxed enough to go to bed, she checked her phone, still no contact from him at all. Tears are now starting to form; she wasn't going to let this bother her. She turned the lights off and went to sleep.

As Harper prepared for work, her phone beeps, "Hey my phone died, I hope you are ok? You left so fast I didn't get a hug or to talk to you about my birthday weekend." She responded, "what about your birthday weekend?

"I want you to come to my birthday workout party." Was the response he sent to her.

She stared at the phone for a few minutes, "Yes, I will be at your party, I am not sure that I am welcome there, but I will attend. I will not be back at your class until your party. I am getting a vibe from Dina that makes me feel like I am interrupting something between you two."

"Please don't start that shit again, there's nothing going on with the two of us. She is married, I think she has kids also. I am not trying to be in the middle of something like that. I look forward to seeing you at my birthday party next week. Are you coming down Sunday?"

Harper took a few minutes to think about what she wanted to say. She wanted to go on Sunday to spend time with him. There is something still not sitting right with her. She replied, since I am spending the weekend with you in a week, I will save the wear and tear on my car and see you next weekend and we can have a good time. Maybe I can cash in on the weekend at the beach that you owe me.

"Sounds good. This is sounding like I am going to have a good birthday; I am so glad that you are going to be a part of it this year." The texting stopped. When Harper arrived at work she talked about her feelings around the last class, with Andi. How Dina approached her about food for his event. He hadn't invited her yet, but Dina made sure that she was there the next week. Again, something doesn't feel right with this situation.

Preparing for next weekend, she picked up his favorite football team sweatshirt, and some other insignificant things to put in his bag. She also placed the orders needed for the food and had a pickup time of 7:30am for all of it. It takes an hour to get there, the 1st class starts at 9:00am. Harper didn't want to walk in during his class with the food and gifts. Andi asked if there was anything she could do to help. She wanted to go with Harper for support, she had a date with the new guy who took the weekend off to spend with Andi.

To see the smile on Andi's face made Harper so happy. She told her that she had it under control, if she could just say a small prayer that everything she is feeling is wrong, and all will be ok is all she really needed right now. Wow! Saturday got here fast.

CHAPTER 6

You are lying

Harper is driving down the highway, looking forward to seeing Justice. This is the first time she was ever invited to any of his parties that took place around his friends. Her heart was full and knew that this year was going to be their year. The year that there were no more secrets, his friends would know exactly what she meant to him.

Harper pulled into a parking spot to make sure that Justice was nowhere around. Seeing that it was safe to go ahead, she pulled closer to the building to unload the car. Everything looked so nice, you could see how proud Harper was of everything she had gotten for Justice's birthday.

Once inside, there was a class going on. There was Lyssa taking the class. She was always full of energy and good vibes. She was yelling to Harper to get her ass over here and take this step class. Harper let out a laugh, and replied, nope I got bad knees. Remember I told you that last class? I will watch while you take the class for both of us.

Harper turned; she felt an uncomfortable feeling behind her. It was Dina standing there with a smirk on her face that soon turned to a smile. Not knowing what or why, Harper begins to tell her of all the items that she got per her request. The cake with a Justice photo on it was Harper's idea.

Dina threw her hands up in the direction of a table off to the side, with the remarks go over there and set up, he will be here soon. Harper hurried over to set up but was feeling extremely uncomfortable but could not figure out why. Friends and customers started to come in to take Justice's class. Harper started to get excited, this was the day she had waited for, that I would get introduced to his friends.

When Justice came through the door his look at Harper was not one of love or happiness, it was a blank stare and a nod. Harper turned her head with a dumb look on her face, expression was "what the hell is that for?" She continued to stand there, making no motion towards him, watching him as he greeted others with a hug or a smile. What did I do to you? I drove almost two hours just to be here with you on your birthday and I get this shit! .

Shake it off Harper, you are reading too much into this, she said. She took her spot in the corner of the class. Yes, out of sight out of mind. Like the rest of the class, she was streaming the class on Yok! Class was going great until Harper's lower back started to bother her. So, she sat the rest of the class out, but continued to record all the fun everyone was having.

At one point, Justice walked past her and shot her a nasty look of disappointment. His class was ending, he was answering questions from those who were in his live stream. Dina told her to go over and get him before he ends his live so that everyone can see his celebration that we have. "we"? I will leave that alone for now.

Harper told Dina that he doesn't like to be interrupted during his classes or lives. She insisted that Harper go over there. Harper walked over, she interrupted to tell him that Dina would like for him to meet her at the table, also do not end your live, she wants everyone to join in. Harper felt sick to her stomach with another nasty look.

Justice hammed it up for everyone, ended his live stream, asked what the hell was that? Harper responded that it was the request of Dina, any issues you have, you take them up with her.

It was time for the second class to start, the music was not playing currently. You could hear conversations throughout the room. Over Harper's right shoulder was Dina and another person talking.

The lady asked Dina, "who is that? Pointing to Harper, Dina's response is someone that I got to bring all Justice's food for his party. Don't worry, she will be gone shortly. Harper turned her head slightly to let the ladies know that she could hear them. Dina yelled at someone to turn the music on, it's too quiet in here.

Lyssa looked at Harper, she could tell that she had heard everything. You could see the pain in Harper's face. It was time to take Lyssa's class, everyone was back to having a fun time. Harper recording and dancing around also having a fun time.

Harper made the remark that she would leave after Lyssa's class, Justice had other plans afterwards, and they wouldn't be able to hang out. Dina asked Harper to go to the club with them later that night. So she wouldn't have to drive back home, she offered for her to stay at her house while we waited, so she wouldn't have to go home and come back.

Why would she even think about going to her house, with the comments, gestures and just being rude. No, Harper was going back home. Class is over, Lyssa and Harper walk over to Justice at the same time. Harper thanked him for the invitation to the party, she had fun and hoped he enjoyed the gifts and food. She gave him a hug, stepped back to leave, when Lyssa said hey, wait for me I will walk out with you.

Lyssa reached in, gave her hugs and goodbye's. As they walked out together, the group started to stare at them. Outside the two talked about how uncomfortable Harper was feeling. Lyssa was feeling the same way, she also heard Dina talking about me to that lady, she shared that Dina had been talking about me the entire time. That's why Lyssa was ready to go, she didn't want any drama.

Harper asked her why would there be any drama? Lyssa got quiet, she looked at Harper, replied you do not know, do you?

Both sat on the side of the rock wall. Lyssa remarked that he is only acting shitty like that because of her. Harper responded no that can't be, she's married, and they are friends. The red flags that Harper had changed to white to say it was safe to be with him have turned red and there's no going back to any other color.

House of Cards
Starts to Crumble

The wind was blowing, it was chilly as Lyssa and Harper continued to sit outside. Harper looked at Lyssa who seemed just as heartbroken as she was, asking how long this had been going on?

Lyssa shrugged her shoulders;" I have no idea" she said. As the two sat there and the wind was blowing, Lyssa finished her snack, but didn't have anywhere to throw it. With rage in her heart Harper looked at Lyssa, "I have the perfect idea, come on let's go back inside and throw your trash away.

I need a drink anyway. Lyssa and Harper went back inside, to see Dina right next to Justice, they both had their backs turned so they did not know that Harper and Lyssa came back to the party.

As soon as Justice turned and saw them both together, he grabbed his phone and sat down. Harper and Lyssa looked at each other laughing and returned outside. As much as they both wanted to laugh, they knew the truth, it was right there in front of both of their faces. The Ladies continued to talk; the things shared made everything a lot clearer for both.

Harper never could get Justice to hang out with her on Friday's he told her, that he was teaching classes and it would be a waste for her to drive down to see him, because she had to leave at 5am to get to work by 6am the next day. They are spending time together on Sunday's after she got off from work.

The real reason was he was with Lyssa on Friday nights. Lyssa now understood why she couldn't see him on Sunday's, he would tell her that he was always training with someone. He was, he had been Dina's personal trainer for the last 6 months. Rage flew into Harper, what the hell? Yes, Lyssa, this all makes sense. You could tell that both ladies were beyond crushed. One of the instructors was leaving the class, she remarked to them both, I thought you two had left, what's up. Harper responded, she left because of the messed up shit that was going on in there. To get this information I am hurt, someone is going to need to hold my ass back.

She agreed that the class was not the same and it had nothing to do with Harper being there. She also stated that you could feel tension in the air, like something was about to go down. They both responded that's why we left. The lady said in a confident voice, don't you guys sweat that mess in there. Karma has a way of coming back when you least expect it.

Harper wanted Karma at that time, not when it suited her! Harper, 3 dam years I put up with the excuses, I was always told that I was reading too much into things, into pictures. No, I was reading too much into Justice.

The ladies had been outside talking for so long that Justice was walking out of the building. He looked over at them both as he got into his car. When he drove past them, he was slumped so far down in the seat you could barely see him.

He pulled up to them both, asked if they were ok, both replied, "oh yeah we are great". Justice drove off with a strange look on his face. Harper yelled, wait one dam moment. Lyssa lifted her head, what? Look at Dina's car that was next to where they were sitting, she replied ok what?

Look at the parking pass in Dina's window. Lyssa response was oh shit! Dina's has one of Justice's parking passes to where he lives.

You could now see the tears in both of their eyes, they went away quickly when they saw Dina leaving the building. Dina is all smiles, asking how long had they been outside? Harper response since they walked out the building, why do you want to know? Dina said, since we were still there, why don't we go to my house, until it was time to go to the club. Lyssa and Harper looked at each other then back at Dina, "Nah we good said Harper.

Dina continued to walk to her car, "come on ladies lets continued the party." Harper again replied, Nah. She had had enough partying for the day and that she was sure that she really did not want her to party with herself and Justice. With a confused look on her face, why would you say that I would not offer for you to come to my house if I didn't?

Oh Really! Replied Harper. Harper glanced over at Lyssa whose eyes were now almost full of tears, as she looked in the other direction. Dina has now gotten into her car, pulled beside them both, what do you mean that I don't seem like I want you to hang around. Harper, Uh the comments you made in the class, I am good.

Looking at Dina in the car, she had her phone positioned, like she was taking photos, but no real reason for her to do so. Harper responded that she and Lyssa were going out later with some of the people from the class. Dina seemed mad but they didn't care. She pulled away making comments under her breath.

The ladies return to talking, both not paying attention to the time or to their phones. Harper grabbed her phone to make sure that none of her family had called. There was a message on there from Justice, "are you still with Lyssa?" "If you are, her son is trying to reach her." Just as she was going to show her the message, Lyssa's mother pulled up.

She was worried about her, her mom seemed to calm down once she saw that she was ok. Lyssa introduced her mother to Harper, she started to share the story with her.

She said, "do you remember I was telling you about one of Justice's friends who was getting text messages, she had to get her phone number changed? This is her."

Harper leans in to speak, she commented how crazy that was. During the time that it was going on the Justice blamed her for sending the text messages. Harper had a dumb look on her face, she said why would I send a message to myself and change a number that I have had for over 10 years.

They both started to share what happened at the party, they both were so bitter, hurt and disgusted. Lyssa's mother said not to worry that everything will play itself out. For them not to do anything drastic. Here stands two young ladies completely devastated at the action of this man.

This man, who had been seeing both ladies for three years. And the more that they talked, this man who was a trainer using the word loosely, covered also sleeping with three other people. Harper leaned against the car, at that moment everything hit like a ton of bricks. How did we get here? What was wrong with me that I was not enough for him? What did they do that I did not do?

The ladies looked over and saw Harper falling to the ground, and they came over to her. Are you ok? No! Harper replied. I just wasted 3 years of my life with someone who really did not love me. How could he say that he loved me and missed me, but the entire time he had a woman at his request any time he wanted one, including ME!

Lyssa tried to make her feel better, she told her that he did care about you. Harper turned to Lyssa; how do you know? Well, you two always went places together, the only place that we would go together would be workout events. She remarked on concerts, beach trips, then she reflected on thanksgiving in New York with Dina, trips to Atlanta with Kourtney and was always at a party with Sherri.

It looks like we had our purpose to Justice. Still doesn't make it any better that this shit is happening to us. In a normal situation the women would have some type of altercations with each other. With Harper and Lyssa, it was the total opposite. As they continued to sit out in the cold, they went from comparing notes, to playing back the years of being with Justice.

The more they talked the more the puzzle pieces started to fit together, and the years wasted all make sense. Did it hurt Harper? Yes, she had to hear it all. Let us go back a little bit, Lyssa said, Harper agreed. Have you met any members of his family? No, Harper replied, have you? "Nope." What reason did you get? Harper looking down at the ground, he told me, that he had had a rough break-up, he wanted to make sure that the next person he brought into his children's life was the person that was going to be there to stay.

For a while I respected that, Harper said. Lyssa remarked that he was being consistent. Harper looking back in her directions, why is it that he always posting pictures of himself and Kourtney? I was getting upset about it, he told me that I was reading too much into pictures. Lyssa looked at Harper, she shook her head, no you were not reading too much into those photos. Everything that you were seeing and feeling was correct about them, they were viewed as a couple. Harper started to cry; he told me that she was just like one of the boys. As much as I knew she wasn't, Harper said, I just chose to believe him and deal with my own insecurities.

The hits just kept coming, Dina posting videos of her in Justice's bed, is this why she had the parking pass? Why would a person do that who had a husband and four kids? Yes, four kids. Lyssa apologized; she thought that Harper knew this. As she really did not, or she did and refused to see it. Harper told her about the concert that they went to just last week. She began to put pieces together. Justice and Lyssa were supposed to go out that Friday, he was with Harper, but told Lyssa that he was going with some friends.

How many more lies can one person tell? How was he able to keep up with everything he was saying? How was it possible that none of us ran into each other until now? Harper's head was spinning until the point she had to sit down. It was time to head home, Lyssa was visibly upset while Harper was trying to hold a tough appearance.

As they separated, Harper takes to social media, she is crying telling the world what just took place. She didn't use Justice's name but those in her circle knew who she was talking about.

It was comforting to her to get the support that she did, she still felt used and taken advantage of. She finally arrives back to her house. Takes a hot shower, wraps up to watch TV, her phones beeps. It was Justice, I want to thank you for ruining my birthday. WTH! I ruined your birthday. What about what you did to us???

You make it out like I said we were in a relationship, I never told you that we were dating. Harper starts to scream at the phone what do you mean? I can't with you right now, Justice go hang out with one of your little tarts and leave me alone. I will talk to you in the morning Justice replies. Whatever says Harper.

CHAPTER 8

What's Next

Later, the phone rang, hey Harper, I am so sorry that I put you through this. You know I love you and want to make it up to you. Can we have dinner at my place on Sunday like we usually do and talk this through? Harper did not respond to the message instead she reached out to Andi; she knew she would tell her what the best solution would be.

Andi's text.

"The only way to get closure is to see him, to see what he has to say about this."

Harper responded, "thanks" then she sent Justice a text, she would see him Sunday.

His response was great. I will fix your favorite meal; we will get through this Harp.

Sunday's here, I know he likes white she says, so she puts on the outfit that she wore when she met him. Stopped at the gas station, to fill up her car, get her energy drink and pretzels for the drive. The weather was beautiful, she had the windows down, music playing. Feeling nothing but positive vibes.

Harper arrived as usual and an hour early, but she wanted to get this out of the way, either they were going to make this work, or she was going to walk away with years of her life wasted.

Knock knock.

Knock, knock, knock.

"What the hell?"

"I know he hears me!"

"I know he is there; I hear music."

Harper turns the doorknob, it is unlocked. She walks in, the table is set for their date. Music is playing, Justice is nowhere in sight.

The music is coming from the back of the apartment, Harper starts to walk in the direction of the music. The closer she gets to the door, the more she realizes this might not be a promising idea.

She stands at the door, on the other side, sounds of someone other than Justice. Harper opens the door, with pain in her heart, there's Justice with three other women in the bed. Harper stands there for what seems to be forever, watching them. There were three women pleasuring Justice, she gasped for air, all four of them stop what they were doing to see her standing in the doorway.

Harper reaches into her bag, grabs her gun as Justice is crawling to the edge of the bed saying it is not what you think. With the gun placed in the middle of Justice's forehead, she replied, this is not what YOU THINK!!!! The gun goes off.

Harper sits up in the bed in a cold sweat, she looks around, she is at home. This was a bad dream, as she pulls herself together, she begins to think. I have thrown away years of my life, what is wrong with me? Why am I not good enough? What did they have that I did not. At that moment rage flew into her, she ripped off the sheets, she pulled all her clothes out of the dresser. She cleared her bathroom countertop with one swoop.

With glass bottles crashing around her, one of the broken bottles landed on her foot. There was a deep gash on her foot where one of the perfume bottles had fallen. Harper was so full of rage, anger and hurt she did not notice that her foot was bleeding. As she turned to continue taking her rage out on her closet, she slipped on the blood covered floor.

Harper is lying in a pool of blood, at that very moment she has reached her darkest point, and the lowest of her lows, sees a piece of glass on the floor. Everything that was going through her mind, she took the glass and put it on her wrist. As she was about to apply pressure, her phone rang. It snapped her out of a trance.

She crawled to her phone that was buried under clothes on the floor. It was Andi.

"Hey, are you ok?"

"Where are you?"

"You have not been at work for a couple of days."

Harper says in a faint voice, "come get me!" "I need to go to the emergency room."

Do not ask questions, hurry up please.

Andi arrives, without a key to the house, she uses the code key for the garage. Once inside, she makes her way towards Harper's bedroom. What she sees is short of a horror movie. Clothes thrown all over the room, broken glass, and blood everywhere. On the bathroom floor lies Harper.

Harper is barely breathing and covered in blood. Andi panics, calls 911. As she is talking to them, Harper tells her to hang up. Andi says no. Harper replies they will put me away. Andi told her that she would make sure that it would not happen.

The EMT arrived, Andi said that she believed that the house was burglarized. Once the EMT heard that, they called the police. As they were putting Harper into the rescue squad, the police arrived. No time to talk to her, they followed her to the hospital to ask questions.

The police, doctors, and Andi were all in the room with Harper, the questions started coming from everyone, all at one time. Harper sits up in bed! I am not crazy, I was Dumped Dumped Dumped, Dumped, Dammit!

Harper continues, I am hurt, embarrassed. I am disappointed in myself. I saw the red flags, I knew they were there, but I chose to change the colors of them to fit my own personal needs. I knew he was cheating; how do you call it cheating when he says that you were never in a relationship? How do you call it cheating, when he says, "I love you." But he will never post a photo of the two of you together.

Yes, those are red flags, did I see them? Yes, yes, I saw every one of them. Again, I say I am not crazy, I don't need someone to lock me up. To put me in a jacket that makes me hug myself. I just need time to understand this mess and find out who I am and what my worth is.

CHAPTER 9

Harper's unknown

The doctors kept Harper overnight, she was sitting on the side of the bed waiting for Andi to pick her up. Two doctors walked into the room along with a nurse and a man, with a police or security officer.

"Good morning Harper, how are you feeling today?" asked the doctor.

"I feel better" responded Harper.

The doctor begins.

"After going over your statement to the police, we feel that you are not able to go home, and you need to stay in a facility for a week for further evaluation."

Harper sat still on the side of the bed, with no response. The nurse began to prepare her for release to the other hospital. Harper's choice was to wear the jacket out or she could wear plastic wrist ties. She picked the wrist ties with the request that they put her jacket over the ties, so they wouldn't bring too much attention to the situation.

The doctor had reached out to Andi, and Elise, both were at the doors of the other hospital when the rescue squad pulled up. The EMT's explained that they can talk to her for a few minutes, but she must go in with no contact for 72 hours. The ladies were more than willing to pick her up when she was released.

Andi and Elise, both hugged her, reminded her that she would be ok. They will be here waiting for her when she walks out. With tears flowing and the ladies unable to compose themselves, the EMT's reached for Harper's elbow to lead her into the building.

The walls were white, the doors were steel. The doors had a small window in them, the size of a tissue box. They continued to walk, Harper came to an abrupt stop. Someone began to scream get me out of here. It was like a domino effect. The entire floor started to yell and scream. Harper wanted to turn and run out of the door, if she did, they would keep her in here for longer than 72 hours.

The EMT's assured her that she was safe, she could keep walking, they were not going to leave her until she was safe in her room, and the doctors were with her. That eased Harper's fears, they turned the corner, it was like going into a different part of the hospital. It now looked more like a hotel than a hospital. You could see Harper's shoulders starting to relax. They reached her room, once inside they took the ties off her wrist, she sat on the side of the bed, staring at them as they left the room.

The only people that came into Harper's room were to deliver meals, one towel that was the size of a kitchen towel, along with half of a washcloth. During dinner, there was a voice over the intercom.

"Harper, how are you feeling?"

"Who the hell is that? Where the hell is that coming from?" she said loudly.

"It's your doctor, Harper." Dr. Royce.

"We have monitored your actions for the last 24 hours; are you ok if we come into your room to talk to you?"

"Yes, that is fine, please do." She replied.

15 minutes later the door opened, in walked a female and male doctor. Harper extended her hand, as did the doctors.

"Nice to meet you both." Said Harper. "So, you all were watching me? That is on some creepy shit, if you don't mind me saying."

"You are correct Harper." Dr. Royce begins to explain. "We have camera's all over your room, we watch our patients the 1st 24 hours to see the reaction that they display, to see how we need to handle treatment."

"So, what does my treatment look like?" Harper asked.

"We have some good news." "If you are ok with this, we would like to talk to you to see what happened to get you here." "We feel that you need outpatient support along with your own bed, you will heal better with this in place" suggested Dr. Royce.

Dr. Gentry added, "while watching you, there was no signs that you wanted to or will hurt yourself." "Instead, you took the time to meditate, exercise. You showed signs of clearing your mind. The plan for tomorrow is to talk about what got you here and what we are going to do."

There was a strange noise from behind the wall. The doctors opened a wall panel that had a TV behind it. Harper was allowed to watch TV. The shows were ones picked by the doctors; she was also able to take a bath instead of a shower. She was able to relax for the night, also to prepare for the next day.

Sun is rising, Harper's breakfast was delivered, the doctors came in right behind the delivery. They both have smiles on their faces, ready to work they asked? Everyone sat comfortably while Harper ate her breakfast; the conversation was light and had nothing to do with the event that took place. Once Harper pushed away her plate, sat back in the chair, the tone turned profoundly serious. "If you can, Harper, please tell us how you got here."

Harper looks up, the tears start to flow. She was assured that there was no judgement, the more she was able to share, the better the plan would be to help her. She took a deep breath and began.

"I have a good friend, who was helping me surf the internet dating app. I thought I had found the one after going through a bunch of crazy people, I didn't. She continued that she had invested a long time into this situation ship to find out that she was one of four that he was seeing and one of two that he was seeing the entire time they had been together."

She continued, "there were so many hurdles to get to his birthday party." She listed everything that happened.

1. Never meeting his family, kids, or friends.
2. Never posting photos of them on his social media pages, yet he has all his female friends in his photos.
3. Always tell her that she is reading too much into the photos that she is seeing.
4. The text messages from his friends, saying that he was sleeping with Kortney.
5. She thought things were changing because of the invitation to his birthday party.

Both doctors were taking notes as she talked. They seemed to stop writing at the same time looked at each other. Dr. Royce asked if it would be ok if they stepped out for a few minutes to discuss a few options. Harper agreed.

It seems like it was forever before they returned. They had one more question for Harper.

"What are you feeling towards him at this moment?"

"I feel disgusted, used, devalued and some strong hatred." Harper replied.

Both doctors looked at each other, gave a slight nod and Dr. Royce began. "You will be released today if you are able to agree to the terms and conditions that we will set in place for you."

1. You will cut off all contact with him.
2. Work on not looking at his social media.
3. You will meet someone we suggest once a week for 3 months. The reason for 3 months, this is the danger zone where is easy to fall back into all habits.
4. You must keep a journal, with an entry every day for the entire 3 months.
5. Pick one or both of your friends to check in with when you feel that you are losing control. Then reach out to the doctor.

"Is this something you think you can manage?" asked Dr. Royce.

Harper's reply was quick, along with a smile. "YES!" I tried to tell them in the Emergency Room, I was ok, I was just dumped and tore my room up. No one wanted to listen to me. I am glad you two did."

The next morning, Andi and Elise were waiting for Harper to walk through the door. Both ladies were so happy to see her and the fact that she was so relaxed looking after two days was great. It was like a scene from the movie with them running to each other. The ladies had a big slumber party at Harper's house, they did not want her alone on her first night home.

Against Andi and Elise's wishes, she returns to work. Harper was there with a smile on her face, her coworkers thought that she was getting better, that was far from the truth. Harper stayed in a deep depression for a while, she worked hard to get through this. Things did not move as fast as she would have liked. She would find herself going home, sitting in the dark watching his social media. Watching Justice post photos of the new or existing chick. One of the things that the doctor's asked her not to do.

She would spend time comparing herself to the new woman. Could she really say new woman? She was one of the four that he saw while dating her. What could I change to make him want me again? Then one day it hit her, all the self-help classes, workbooks and talks with friends, there is nothing wrong with her. In that moment she vowed she would focus on herself. She would get herself to a good place with her self-care, her self-worth before she would even think about seeing anyone again.

Harper is now going out with friends, Friday nights, the ladies would find themselves at different clubs around the metropolitan area. Her friends could not figure out why she was hanging out with Lyssa, they would soon see that she was a good person. That this situation was not her fault. It was Justice's fault they were put in that predicament. It did not take long before they all became friends.

The ladies have been working hard not to pay attention to what was happening in their life. The harder that they would work to remove those two from their lives, the more they would find their way in. Stalking both of their social medias, showing up at the same events, they would attend. Lyssa dealt with a lot of negative back lash from Dina.

They both were in the same social circles; Dina would have negative things to say about Lyssa. Those negative comments would get back to her, one day she was told of one comment that upset her so bad she took to social media. Harper watched; she became upset too. Dina is telling the world that she is running behind Justice, making fake calls, and threatening her.

Harper called to interrupt her live on social media. She reminded her of the big picture, that when they are successful that would hurt them more than responding to her childish crap. Harper started to notice that she was no longer checking his social media pages. Yet Justice is now on her social media pages, liking her photos. Why is he on my page? She sent a screen shot to Lyssa, and she was hitting send with her screen shots, Lyssa was sending hers. Both started to laugh via text message.

Harper suggested blocking them, Lyssa response "HELL NO!"

Let them see the glow-up. Harper waited a few minutes, then she agreed not to block them.

CHAPTER 10

Life's looking good

This was the best both ladies have felt in a long time. When Harper would get down, Lyssa would call or text her so she wouldn't have to worry Andi and Elise, Harper did the same for Lyssa. One thing that did come out of this mess was a friendship that would last.

Harper gave herself a solid year before she would go out with anyone, it's time to let the healing process begin. Harper was still very bitter, Lyssa and herself worked together to support each other. They would still run into their friends, who thought that this was a little strange that the women are friends.

Why wouldn't you be? It has always been the normal, that the woman goes after each other. If they would take the time to talk, they would realize that it is the man that is in the center of the issues. Yes, Harper and Lyssa are now friends. It does not sit well with Justice that they are spending time together. Neither one of them really cared what he thought. He had made up his mind who he wanted.

Harper called Lyssa, she said she wanted to write a book about what they had gone through. Do you think it would be something people would want to read? She was sure that there's not too many stories of one man, and four women. She always wanted to do something to help others, So why not become a life coach? Harper had a plan, Lyssa supported Harper's idea along with her visions to become a Life Coach to help others who have gone through the same thing.

Lyssa is ready to go back to teaching classes and putting all her energy into her brand. Exercise is her life she wasn't going to let Justice and Dina stop her from doing what she wanted to do. They made a deal that they would push each other to be the best versions of themselves that they can be. They promised each other that all the photos, and social media clapback's they would not let those things get to them.

Lyssa had struggles with how to get her plans together. The two of them made a bond that they would be each other's support. Lyssa began to throw herself into her job, and the projects she had going. A month later, Lyssa's exercise classes began to take off. She had classes all over the metropolitan area. When you thought things couldn't get better for Lyssa, she started to teach classes in other states.

Harper was so proud of her new friend, they were having lunch together, when Lyssa shared her good news. She will be a lead exercise teacher for a major brand in the metropolitan area. She will have an online presence and her in-person classes. While they celebrated Lyssa's good news, they both agreed that this was a good time for them.

Harper also was sitting on good news, she looked at Lyssa, it was my turn. "I GOT A BOOK DEAL!" The party is getting better with all the good news, they both are heading to a good place and the past is starting to become just that, the past. Harper starts to travel; she is posting her photos of the good times she is having without Justice.

She noticed that Justice is on her social media pages, liking her post, commenting on them. A rage flew into Harper that she had not felt in a long time. At that moment, she called Lyssa to tell her what was going on. He has been on Lyssa's pages also.

Lyssa yells on the phone why is he doing this, Dina has been on my page also. He got what he wanted, he has her, their new business, and the family he always wanted. He needs to leave us the hell alone. Harper says should we block him now? Nope, Lyssa says, he must be unhappy and now realized what he had and wants us back.

Harper started to laugh, she remarked "I have worked too hard to get to this point in my life. I finally feel the best I have in years. He has no place in my life anymore. I will sit back and let karma take care of this hot mess."

The ladies started to notice that Justice was not the same person he was when he was with them. He was also starting to dress like Dina, they both would always have on the same color. He was never anywhere without her. Everything that he said he would not do; he was doing with her. When the camera would catch her, it was like she had a death stare on him, and he was scared to say or do anything.

Harper almost felt sorry for him, but that feeling lasted a good 30 seconds. She was sure that he did not feel bad, when she was hurting, when she was in one of the darkest places of her life. He could rot in the living hell that he has created for his life.

Looking at how the women who he has hurt are doing now, there is not one ounce of feeling for him anymore. Kourtney now has a striving business, what if this did not happen, she would still be in his shadow, just being Tina to his Ike. Lyssa is a sought-after exercise instructor. Harper has written a book and become a life coach. Dina has him right where she wants him. Harper wishes them nothing but the best and wants him to leave her the hell alone, stay off her social media pages and find a life.

As the healing was starting for Lyssa and Harper, they were out one night at a club, Lyssa's son ran in to get her. At first, we thought something had happened to her mother the way he came in. He never said a word, only that we needed to leave. Something has happened that we both needed to see.

The ladies ran out of the club, in the parking lot waiting, was Lyssa's mother. "Hop in, hurry up, there's been an accident, you two need to get there quickly." Harper's heart dropped; she thought something had happened to one of the girls that would meet them at the club. Did Andi try to come to the club and was in a wreck? Harper yells "hurry we need to make sure our girls are ok!"

Lyssa's mom turned around with a strange look, "your girls?" She came to a sudden stop, we were at a bridge, there was a police barricade set up. The police officers are putting up caution tape everywhere. Just as Harper was going to ask another question BOOM! Coming from beneath the bridge was large red & orange flames shooting to the skies. Lyssa's mom turned back around she repeated, "your girls? No that's Justice, who went over that bridge."

Both Lyssa and Harper screamed at the same time, NOOOOOOOOOOOOOO!!!!! They jumped out of the car and ran as close to the edge as they could. Harper looked to her right, two feet away was Dina looking down at his car in flames. Lyssa hits Harper's arm, she pointed to the left of her. There stood Kourtney, she too was looking down at his burning car.

There stood, all 4 women that Justice had been with, standing 2 feet apart from each other. No one was sure what was going through their minds. This is the first time that they are all in the same place together. Lyssa's mom prepared the police for what could be an ugly situation. It was in slow motion that they all raised their hands and pointed to the car and screamed LOOK!!!!!

With guns drawn, the police started to run towards the ladies, as the fire department extinguished the fire, they all stood in complete shock at what was at the bottom of the hill. Firefighters gestured for the police to come down the hill, to look at the car.

They all looked at each other, then the police yelled to the top of the hill.

"Where is he?"

Epilogue

"911 how can I help you?"

"there's a man walking on the highway that looks like he's been in a house fire."

"911 how can I help you?"

"there's a man walking on highway 24 he looks drunk and like someone has set him on fire."

6 police cars are flying down highway 24 looking for this man. For an hour they searched the area where this man was seen, nothing. They radioed back if they get another call like that, please get the location that they are calling from, the search continues.

While all of this is going on, Reya is out for her afterwork jog. She jogs every night after work on a well light trail with night monitors. Reya has moved to the metropolitan area from Hawaii. Reya works at the college campus as a nurse intern, also at the hospital as an on call emergency nurse intern.

Right before she entered the monitored trail, she noticed feet under a bush, she stopped to check out what was going on. There's a man lying in the shrubs, clothes are burned, his body is charred. Her first reaction was to yell for help. Just as she was about to, he raised his hand to gesture, stop. She leaned in to hear what he was saying,

"Take me…………take me to your house, please!" the man asked.

"You need help, you need to go to the hospital." Reya said in a frantic manner.

"NO! take me to your house, I am begging you.!"

Reya helped him up, they walked a block to her apartment. Once in the apartment her nursing instincts kicked in. She placed him in the tub, cut his clothes off and gently cleaned his wounds. She worked with urgency to make sure that he did not go into shock.

Once the wounds were cleaned, she moved him to the sofa, to cover him with blankets. He was starting to shiver, due to lack of clothing. After several glasses of water, and electrolyte drinks, he was talking a little.

She asked what happened to him? With a low raspy voice, he was going around a curve, he pushed the brakes, the car wouldn't stop. He went off a bridge, was ejected from the car. When the car hit the bottom of the hill it burst into flames, that's how I got these burns.

I was climbing back to the street, when I saw the women from my past and present standing at the top of the hill. At first, I was happy to see them all there, that meant that they still cared about me, right? As I continued back up the ditch (he starts again with the heavy coughing) I started to think about how I got down here. Are they here to make sure I am, ok? Or are they here to make sure I died? I rolled back down the hill, I crawled into a drain until the police and firefighters left the area.

He is starting to cough more; Reya goes to get him more water.

"We need to call the police to let them know what you think happened so that they can investigate." She remarks.

"No! I will handle this one on my own." He says with firmness.

"I am going to take care of them one at a time!"

"Kourtney"

"Harper"

"Lyssa"

"Dina"

"And you are going to help with each one of them!"

Reya is afraid of him, the way he is talking about taking care of these women. Her voice now shaking as she speaks.

"What do you have planned for them?"

He stares at the ceiling for a few minutes, turns to her with a simple response.

"REVENGE!"

"JUSTICE REVENGE!"

9 781953 163776